Happy Birthday
James and Kate
Love, Anita

Praise for *It's My Time to Fly*

"This beautifully illustrated little book reminds children and their grownups that we aren't all the same, and that's okay. With a little boost from friends and some patience, Caterpillar Number Five makes their own way, on their own time."

—Katja Rowell MD, feeding specialist, and author of
Helping Your Child with Extreme Picky Eating

"*It's My Time to Fly* represents everything wonderful about children's books. It's fun. It's perfectly paced. It reminds of an important truth: not everyone takes the same path, and that's okay. Julie has done a wonderful job telling this story."

—Chris Lassiter, author, journalist, freelance writer

"The character Caterpillar Number Five reinforces a singular truth that every parent or teacher of a child with special needs must finally embrace: that to love that child fully means to meet them where they are each day in their journey with the message, 'I am here . . . right beside you, lifting you up, clearing the path . . . trusting that whatever pace you take on this journey is the right one for you.' Living in that space turns acceptance to celebration and resolution to joy. It is what every child deserves from us."

—Christine Jones, parent, educator, child advocate

"A beautiful story of resilience and triumph at your own pace."

—Leslie Schilling, MA, RAN, dietician, and author of *Born to Eat*

IT'S MY TIME TO FLY

THE STORY OF CATERPILLAR NUMBER FIVE

WRITTEN BY JULIE CONNER
ILLUSTRATED BY EMILY ROW

Brandylane
Publishers, Inc.
Publishing books since 1985

Copyright © 2021 by Julie Conner

No part of this book may be reproduced in any form or by any electronic or mechanical means, or the facilitation thereof, including information storage and retrieval systems, without permission in writing from the publisher, except in the case of brief quotations published in articles and reviews. Any educational institution wishing to photocopy part or all of the work for classroom use, or individual researchers who would like to obtain permission to reprint the work for educational purposes, should contact the publisher.

ISBN: 978-1-951565-83-1
LCCN: 2020921812

Designed by Michael Hardison
Production managed by Haley Simpkiss

Printed in the United States of America

Published by
Brandylane Publishers, Inc.
5 S. 1st Street
Richmond, Virginia 23219

brandylanepublishers.com

To all the caterpillars making their way,
especially my favorite two, Ella & Jake.
I love watching you grow and can't wait to see
the beautiful butterflies you will become . . .
when it's your time to fly!

Once, there were five baby caterpillars.

Those caterpillars grew and grew!

And a little later, with a boost from some friends, he did.

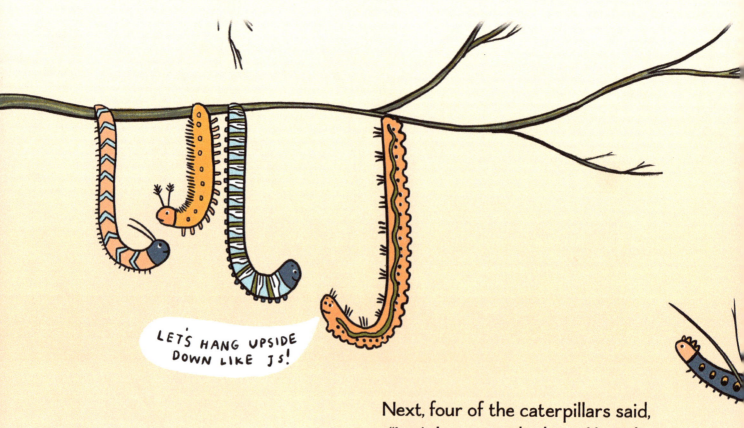

Next, four of the caterpillars said, "Let's hang upside down like Js!"

But Caterpillar Number Five said,
"I will hang like a J . . . when it's my time."

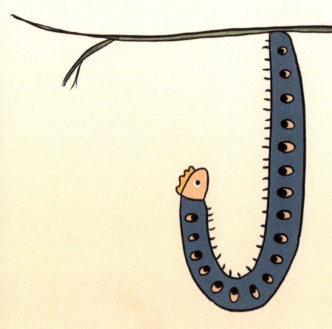

And after some time, he did.

Then, four of the caterpillars said, "It's time to change! Let's get into our chrysalises."

And long after the others, in the wee hours of night, he did.

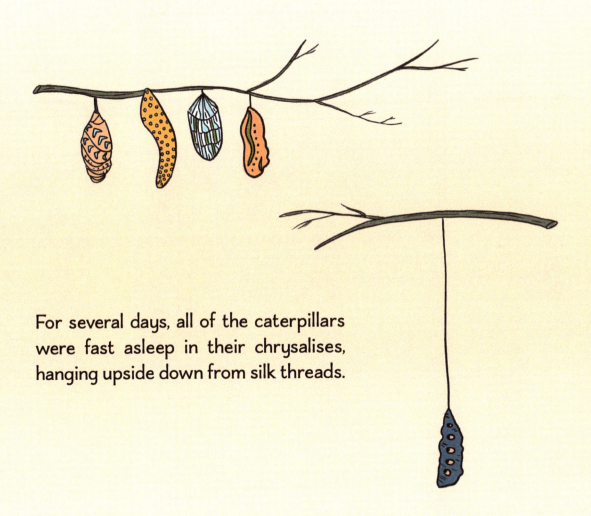

For several days, all of the caterpillars were fast asleep in their chrysalises, hanging upside down from silk threads.

But because Caterpillar Number Five made his thread much longer than the others, it was more fragile and broke away.

While he was sleeping, Caterpillar Number Five fell and landed in the flowers below.

Days went by, and finally four of the caterpillars were ready to wake up and dry off their new butterfly wings.

But Caterpillar Number Five continued to rest in the flowers.

Then, the four butterflies said,
"Now, it's time to fly!"
And they spread their beautiful wings
and flew away into the sunset.

But Caterpillar Number Five was lying in the dirt on his side, squirming and struggling.

So his friends found a rock and helped prop him up, so he would be upside down again.

And the next day, Caterpillar Number Five
—now Butterfly Number Five—
woke up, dried off his new wings, and said,
"Now, it's MY time to fly!"

And in a different place than the other butterflies,
in his own time, with a little help along the way,
he too was able to spread his beautiful wings
and fly away into the sunset.

Careful thought was put into naming Caterpillar Number Five. He was not to be "The Last Caterpillar," or "The Fifth Caterpillar," or anything to indicate that he was lesser or below the rest. He was simply Number Five; on a different path, but changing and developing, all in his own time.

About the Author

Julie Conner has been a special education teacher for eighteen years. She has taught students at various age/grade levels with a wide range of abilities, in multiple school settings, including public schools, a psychiatric care facility, and a school for the deaf and the blind. She has received national recognition from the Council of Schools and Services for the Blind as an Outstanding Teacher of Students who are Blind/Multiply Impaired. Julie lives with her husband and their two children.

It's My Time to Fly: The Story of Caterpillar Number Five was inspired by a butterfly kit gifted to her son. In observing the caterpillars, Julie was amazed to notice that one caterpillar was developing exactly one day later than the others—doing things in his own time, as she had observed was often necessary for her own students and children. She truly hopes this book will be an inspiration to others, imparting the message that it is okay for metamorphosis to take place at an individual pace!

About the Illustrator

Emily Row is an illustrator and garden educator living in the Shenandoah Valley. Her work aims to highlight the beauty in everyday life and objects. Themes of nature and wit are prominent in her illustrations, which are carefully inked or digitally rendered. Her work can be found in local shops around Staunton, Virginia, as well as her online store.

CPSIA information can be obtained
at www.ICGtesting.com
Printed in the USA
BVHW090200110221
599770BV00002B/5